GILBERTO AND THE WIND

BY MARIE HALL ETS

GILBERTO

I am *Gilberto*
and this is the story
of me and the Wind

AND THE WIND

Puffin Books

My thanks to Gilberto

and his mother — and

to Pepe, too — for helping

me make this book

PUFFIN BOOKS
Published by the Penguin Group
Penguin Putnam Books for Young Readers, 345 Hudson Street,
New York, New York 10014, U.S.A.
Penguin Books Ltd, 27 Wrights Lane, London W8 5TZ, England
Penguin Books Australia Ltd, Ringwood, Victoria, Australia
Penguin Books Canada Ltd, 10 Alcorn Avenue, Toronto, Ontario, Canada M4V 3B2
Penguin Books (N.Z.) Ltd, 182-190 Wairau Road, Auckland 10, New Zealand

Penguin Books Ltd, Registered Offices: Harmondsworth, Middlesex, England

First published by The Viking Press 1963
Viking Seafarer Edition published 1969
Reprinted 1971, 1973, 1976
Published in Puffin Books 1978

41 42 43 44 45

Copyright © Marie Hall Ets, 1963
All rights reserved

ISBN 978-0-14-050276-3
Library of Congress catalog card number: 77-18449

Printed in the United States of America

I hear Wind whispering at the door. *"You-ou-ou,"* he whispers.
"You-ou-ou-ou!" So I get my balloon, and I run out to play.

At first Wind is gentle and just floats my balloon around in the air.
But then, with a jerk, he grabs it away and carries it up to the top

of a tree. "Wind! Oh, Wind!" I say. "Blow it back to me! *Please!*"
But he won't. He just laughs and whispers, *"You-ou-ou-ou!"*

Wind loves to play with the wash on the line. He blows the pillow slips into balloons and shakes the sheets and twists the apron strings.

And he pulls out all the clothespins that he can. Then he tries on the clothes—though he knows they're too small.

And Wind loves umbrellas. Once when I took one out in the rain

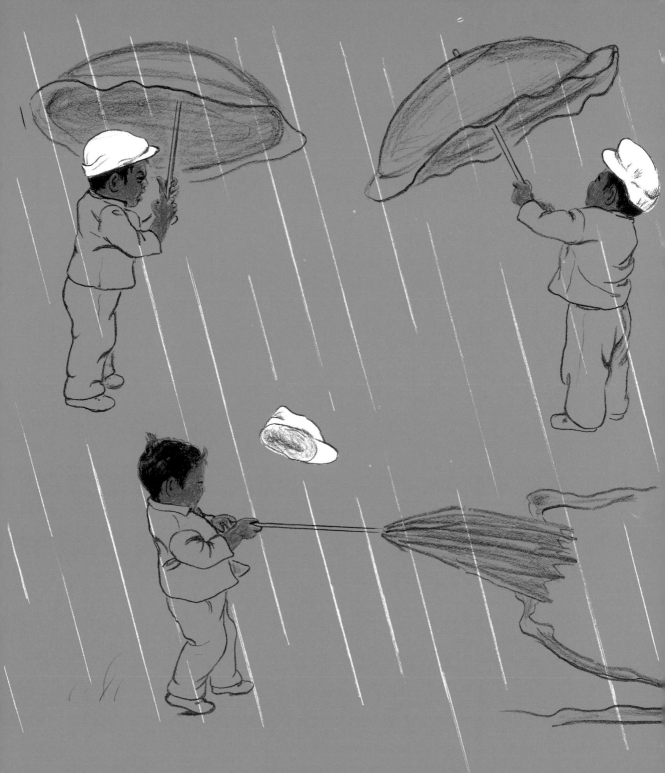

he tried to take it away from me. And when he couldn't, he broke it.

If the gate in the pasture is left unlatched, Wind plays with that, too.
He opens it up, then bangs it shut, making it squeak and cry.

"Wind! Oh, Wind!" I say, and I go and climb on. "Give me a ride!"
But with me on it the gate is too heavy. Wind can't move it at all.

When the grass is tall in the meadow Wind and I like to race. Wind
runs ahead, then comes back and starts over. But he always wins,

because he just runs over the top of the grass and I have to run through it and touch the ground with my feet.

When the big boys on the hill have kites to fly Wind helps *them* out.
Wind carries *their* kites way up to the sky and all around.

But when *I* have a kite Wind won't fly it at all. He just drops it.

"Wind! Oh, Wind!" I say. "I don't like you today!"

When the apples are ripe in the fall, I run with Wind to the pasture

and wait under the tree. And Wind always blows one down for me.

And when I have a boat with a paper sail Wind comes and sails it

for me — just as he sails *big* sailboats for sailors on the sea.

And when I have a pinwheel Wind comes and plays, too. First I
blow it myself to show him how. Then I hold it out, or hold it up,

and Wind blows it for me. And when he blows it, he turns it so fast that it whistles and sings, and all I can see is a blur.

Wind likes my soap bubbles best of all. *He* can't make the bubbles
—*I* have to do that. But he carries them way up into the air for the

sun to color. Then he blows some back and makes me laugh when
they burst in my eyes or on the back of my hand.

When the leaves have fallen off the trees I like to sweep them into
a pile. But then Wind comes along. And just to show that he can

sweep without a broom, Wind scatters the leaves all about again.
And he blows the dirt in my face.

Sometimes Wind is so strong he starts breaking the trees and
knocking down fences. Then I'm afraid. I run in the house and

lock the door. And when Wind comes howling after me and tries
to squeeze in through the keyhole, I tell him, "No!"

But then comes a day when Wind is all tired out. "Wind," I
whisper. "Oh, Wind! Where are you?" "Sh-sh-sh-sh," answers
Wind, and he stirs one dry leaf to show where he is. So I lie down
beside him and we both go to sleep—under the willow tree.